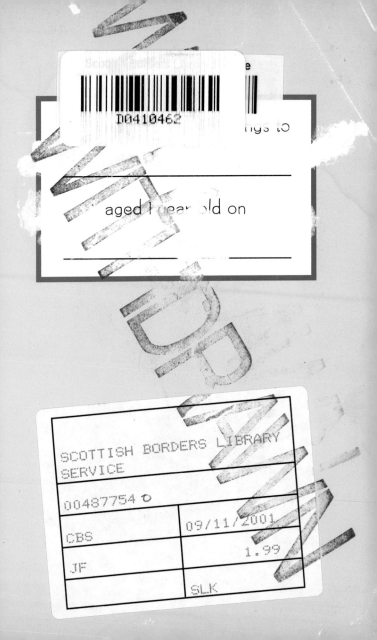

Contents

A catalogue record for this book is available from the British Library

Published by Ladybird Books Ltd
80 Strand London WC2R 0RL
A Penguin Company

2 4 6 8 10 9 7 5 3 1

© LADYBIRD BOOKS LTD MCMLXXXIX / MCMXCIV. This edition MMI

LADYBIRD and the device of a Ladybird are trademarks of Ladybird Books Ltd

Storytime for

1

year olds

by Joan Stimson

illustrated by Nick Spender

Ladybird

Sally and Sam go shopping

Sally and Sam are shopping with their Mum. Mum is pushing a big trolley.

"Don't play with the toilet rolls," Mum tells Sam. "They might run away."

"Don't play with the eggs," Mum tells Sally. "They might break."

When they get home, Mum opens a bag of balloons.

"PUFF, PUFF, PUFF!" Mum blows as hard as she can. She gives a red balloon to Sally and a blue one to Sam.

"NOW," says Mum, "you can play... AS MUCH AS YOU LIKE!"

The lost sock

Lucy has lost one of her socks.
She can't find it anywhere.

It isn't in her bedroom.
It isn't in the bathroom.

It isn't in the kitchen.
It isn't in the hall.

"Where IS that silly old sock?"
Lucy asks Teddy.

"THERE it is!" she cries.
"It's on YOUR foot. And it's been there...
ALL THE TIME!"

By myself

Ben is at the park with Dad. He climbs up the steps to the slide.

"Catch me!" cries Ben, when he reaches the top. WHEEEEE! Ben whizzes down the slide and Dad catches him.

Ben runs over to the swings.

"Lift me up and push me!" cries Ben. SWISH, SWOOSH! Dad pushes Ben backwards and forwards.

The ice cream van comes to the park. DING-A-LING! Dad buys an ice cream for Ben.

"Shall I help you?" asks Dad.

"No, thank you," says Ben. "I can eat it ALL... BY MYSELF!"

Can you touch?

Can you touch your tummy?

Can you touch your toes?

Can you touch your eyes and ears?

Now, what about your... NOSE?

I want to drive

I want to drive a tractor...

I want to drive a train...

I want to drive a big, red bus...

Then FLY home in a plane!

Brand new tooth

Can you see my brand new tooth,
Brand new tooth, brand new tooth?
Can you see my brand new tooth?
It's VERY new and white!

Can you FEEL my brand new tooth,
Brand new tooth, brand new tooth?
Can you FEEL my brand new tooth?
I GREW IT IN THE NIGHT!

Sneezes

Someone needs a tissue,

Someone's going to sneeze.

ATISHOO! ATISHOO!

Pass a tissue please.

Disappearing ducks

Quackety, quackety, quack!
Why DON'T the ducks come back?

Quackety, quackety, HEY!
Why DO they run away?

Cake

This is the cake
Straight out of the tin.

This is the cake
With currants in.

This is the cake,
The very last one.

Let's EAT the cake –
Look... ALL GONE!

Yes! Yes!

"MOO, MOO," says the cow
As she sits in the sun.

"BAA, BAA," says the lamb
"I'm having such fun!"

"WOOF, WOOF," says the dog
As she waits by the door.

"MEOW, MEOW," says the cat
"I'm washing my paw."

"COME IN," calls Dad
As he stands by the sink.

"YES! YES!" cries the girl,
"We ALL need a drink!"

Bathtime

If toes were little fishes
And the bath a great big sea,
Then TEN little fishes
Would be swimming after...

MEEE!

Hugs

Would you like to hug a hippo?

Would you like
to hug a croc?

Would you like to hug an ELEPHANT?
I think you'd get a shock!

Would you like to hug a panda?

Would you like
to hug a sheep?

Would you like to hug your
TEDDY BEAR?...

IT'S TIME TO GO TO SLEEP!